Based on the motion picture screenplay by David Koepp
Based on the novel THE LOST WORLD by Michael Crichton

Dr. Ian Malcolm took a deep breath and stepped off the ocean barge at the edge of a tropical lagoon. He watched as the trailer backed down a narrow ramp. Nick Van Owen, the video documentarian, and Eddie Carr, the equipment specialist, were the only other people involved in this expedition. They were here to observe and record dinosaur life on the island. Ian was here to find Sarah.

Sarah Harding was a paleontologist sent to Isla Sorna by John Hammond, the creator of Jurrassic Park, to study the behavior of dinosaurs on this lost world. Sarah was also Ian's girlfriend. When Hammond told him Sarah was on Isla Sorna, Ian decided to go there and get her out. Ian knew the danger she was in.

And now, to make matters worse, his daughter Kelly had stowed away, hoping for adventure and determined to spend time with her father. "Some adventure," Ian muttered, shaking his head.

As the barge pulled away, the small party made their way into the jungle. They hadn't traveled far when they spotted Sarah. She had been observing a herd of Stegosaurs and now one of the babies in the group was busy observing Sarah. As they joined her, they heard the roar of helicopters. InGen had arrived.

InGen was a company dedicated to one thing — making money. They had come to the island to capture the dinosaurs in order to create a dinosaur zoo. Ian, Kelly, Sarah, Nick and Eddie set out in the direction the choppers had gone.

They came to a ridge overlooking a field and looked down to see what looked like some kind of high-tech dinosaur rodeo. Specially fit trucks were racing through the field, chasing dinosaurs and trying to rope them in. As they watched in horror, one of the hunters managed to rope a young Pachycephalosaurus. Another hunter shot it with a tranquilizer gun, and within minutes, the stunned Pachycephalosaurus had been loaded into a cage and the chase resumed.

As the day wore on, more and more dinosaurs were captured. One of the hunters even managed to catch a baby T-Rex, which was taken back to the InGen base camp and chained to a stake in the hopes that it would attract the most valuable prey of all — an adult Tyrannysaurus Rex.

Later that night, Sarah and Nick sneaked into the InGen camp to free the trapped dinosaurs. As the hunters slept, Nick cut through chains and Sarah opened cage doors. All of a sudden, the animals were loose. In their panic, the dinosaurs tore through the camp, trampling tents and equipment. The hunters scrambled for cover.

Sarah and Nick were headed back to their camp when they spotted the baby T-Rex. As Sarah bent to free the creature, she noticed that its leg had been broken. "We have to do something, Nick," she whispered. "If this bone isn't set , it will never heal properly. He won't survive!"

Nick picked up the screaming baby T-Rex and they ran for their trailer. "He's too loud! He's going to wake the whole jungle," Nick warned as they raced into the trailer with the howling animal.

"He's in pain. It won't take long to get the leg set. Then we'll let him go," said Sarah, and she began to splint the infant dinosaur's broken bone.

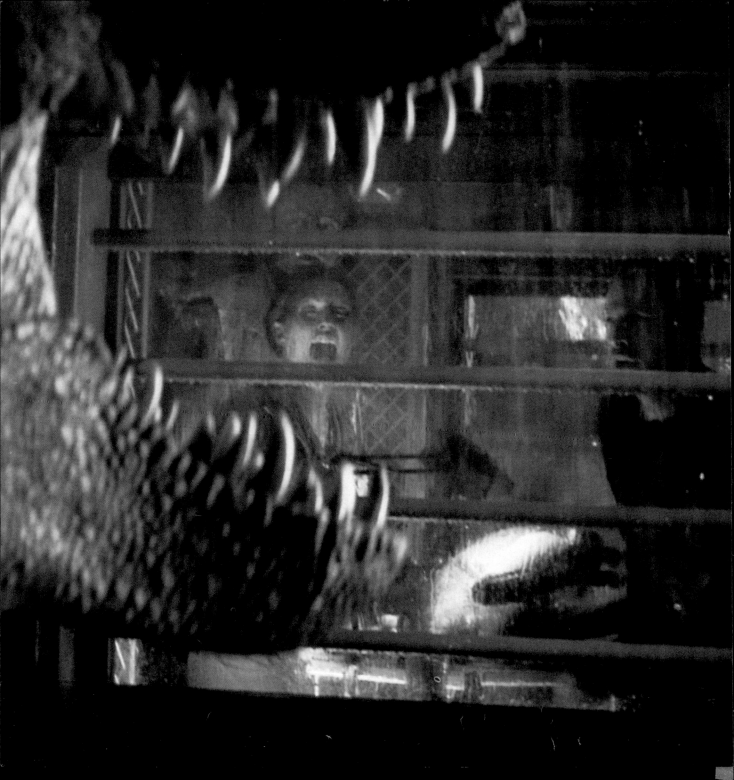

Just as Sarah put the last of the adhesive on the splint, the trailer began to shake. Ian ran into the trailer. "Get that thing out of here! Now!"

"What is it?" Sarah asked.

"It's Mommy and Daddy," Ian told her as he grabbed the small, struggling dinosaur and ran to the door. Two adult T-Rexes were just outside, roaring for their baby as they looked into the trailer windows.

Ian quickly opened the door. The small dinosaur struggled out of his arms, onto the ground and began to gurgle. When the adult T-Rexes saw the baby, they began to gurgle as well, and the three dinosaurs moved off into the jungle together. They sighed with relief.

"It's time to get out of here," Ian said, waiting for an argument. Nick looked at him. "I agree."

"Me, too," Sarah nodded. "Let's find Kelly and Eddie and go home."

Nick turned on the radio to signal the boat to pick them up. Then the trailer began to shake. The T-Rexes weren't finished with them yet. Before Ian could send the signal, there was a huge crash. The trailer turned on its side and began to move. "They're pushing us!" Ian yelled. "And we're headed straight for the cliff!"

Just then, Eddie appeared outside the broken windshield of the fallen trailer. "They haven't seen me," he whispered. "Take the end of this rope. I've tied it to a tree."

All three grabbed the rope just as the trailer slid from the cliff to the rocks below. The T-Rexes turned back for the jungle and saw Eddie. Before he could even try to run, one of them seized him in its mouth and tossed him in the air. As he screamed, both giant heads flashed, and in a split-second, he disappeared between their teeth. Then the two dinosaurs moved off into the jungle.

Sarah, Nick and Ian clung to the rope, dangling above the smashed trailer. They slowly began to pull themselves up when suddenly, a hand appeared over the edge of the cliff. It was one of the hunters. He pulled them to safety where Kelly was waiting, her eyes wide with fear. Without speaking, they followed the hunter back to what was left of the InGen base camp.

Neither of the groups had any equipment left. It had all been destroyed by the dinosaurs. They had no radio to signal for help. But they had a map. On the interior of the island was a small village. It was deserted now, mostly destroyed by a hurricane, but it held a communication station — and a radio. The weary survivors set out on the long journey to the village.

After several hours of walking through the thick jungle, the ground began to tremble again. The territorial T-Rexes had decided that they didn't want these humans on their island anymore.

Everyone in the party scattered, running through the jungle to escape the angry dinosaurs. They reached a ravine with the T-Rexes close behind. As they ran in terror, Nick saw a waterfall with a strange opening behind it. He grabbed Kelly and Sarah and they ran to the waterfall.

"Jump!" Nick yelled, and they all leapt into the falling water — and through it — into a tiny cave. They pressed to the back of the cave as the dinosaur chase continued, holding their breath as they heard the terrified screams of the unlucky hunters who were unable to escape the wrath of the mighty T-Rexes.

After a long while, the jungle outside grew quiet again. Sarah, Nick and Kelly stepped back out into the ravine and saw Ian. He hugged Kelly and thanked Nick. The hunters who had survived the attack were long gone. Now they were alone.

As Ian, Kelly, Sarah and Nick were making their way through the jungle, the remaining hunters were still running. Finally they stopped at the edge of a field of tall grass, laughing with relief. Around them, all was still. They had survived.

The small band of men began to cross through the field in a single file line, blindly pushing at grass taller than themselves.

Silently, a head rose above the grass. Then another. And another. This was the nesting ground of the Velociraptors. On all sides, the grass rippled as the raptors moved swiftly and silently toward their prey.

The last hunter in line suddenly disappeared without a noise. The group moved on, not knowing the danger they were in. The next hunter disappeared as suddenly as the first, then the next. The hunter at the head of the line turned to the man behind him, only to see a Velociraptor springing out of the grass at him. He screamed for a second. Then all was silent. It was, once more, a quiet, peaceful field.

Ian, Kelly, Nick and Sarah reached the clearing at the end of the grassy field and started through it. They hadn't gone far when Ian heard a familiar snarl and he saw the tall grass shivering.

"Run! Run as fast as you can! Go!" he shouted, and they raced blindly through the field. Suddenly the ground disappeared beneath their feet and they were tumbling down a steep, rocky hillside.

When they got to the bottom, Nick got to his feet shakily and dusted off his pants as he looked around. They were just outside the village. "Are you guys alright?" he asked, offering Sarah a hand.

"No," said Ian. "I really messed up my leg." His leg was twisted at an odd angle beneath him.

"Nick, you go ahead," Sarah told him. "You're the fastest runner of all of us. Get to the communication center and radio for help. Kelly and I will stay with Ian."

Nick shot off into the darkness as Ian slowly and painfully got to his feet. He leaned on Sarah for support and the three of them headed in the direction Nick had gone. They hadn't gone far when there was a blinding light. The communication station was lit like a beacon just ahead. Ian, Kelly and Sarah sighed with relief.